The Hidden Enemy

The Griffins of Elderwood

Janet Racciato

DEDICATION

I dedicate this story to first responders. To all the men and women who risk their lives to protect us I'd like to say, Thank you.

ACKNOWLEDGMENTS

I'd like to acknowledge my fellow writer's and teachers who helped me write this series. Your advice and critiques really helped me develop and improve my writing.

CHAPTER 1

"Toric's here," Marsh pushed her bedroom door open.

"Okay," Chiara took one last look around her room.

"Are you ready?" Marsh asked quietly.

Chiara knew this was hard for her dad. After her mother died, she was the only family he had left. "I think so." She tried to smile, but it came out lopsided. This was the first time she'd ever left their small town of Farebrook.

Neither of them spoke as they walked through the house. Chiara noticed things that she'd never paid attention to. Little things, like how the wood floor was polished smooth from the shoes of all the generations of their family who had lived there. Already getting homesick, she reminded herself that she'd be back soon,.

The sturdy farm door stood open. Late fall sunlight, slanted across the floor of their front room. She could hear people talking outside.

"Zae, tell that griffin of yours to stay back," Chiara recognized Toric's grumble. "He's making my horse nervous."

"Of course, sir," Zae answered quickly.

"I've been worried with how

the town was reacting to these beasts," The town's Man-at-Arms mused. "I haven't thought about how the animals liked them."

"Cirrus didn't mean to cause trouble," Zae explained. "He's just never seen a horse up close."

"It's alright." Toric wiped his face with his hand and sighed. "I just hope the oxen don't give us a problem today."

"The griffins don't need to be close to us." Chiara stepped out from the farmhouse door. She spotted Zae shooing his griffin further away from Toric. Cirrus was still craning his large, birdlike head around Zae's shoulder to get a look at Toric's horse. The white feathers of his head contrasted with the stormy grey fur of the rest of his body.

"They don't?" Toric's his face brightened. "Then how do you give them commands?"

"Well, we don't really give them commands," Chiara began. "We just have to think about what we want."

"Huh," Toric grunted. "When we have more time you'll have to explain that better. Right now we need to get moving. I told the wagons to start lining up."

"So hurry and mount up," Zae teased her. "We don't want to keep them waiting forever."

"I love you, Dad." Chiara gave her father one last hug. She felt her eyes threaten to fill with tears

"Be careful," Marsh told her. When their eyes met she saw worry in his hazel eyes.

"I'll have her back to you in a

fortnight," Toric reassured him. "Safe and sound."

Marsh gave Chiara a boost up into the saddle. Jeter, her old gelding, stood with his ears pricked forward, stomping his foot impatiently.

Jeter had been a cavalry horse when he was younger. When he was too old for battle her father had traded a new saddle for the red buckskin. Since then he'd had an easy life rounding up livestock. Today, he could sense something was happening.

Marsh checked the straps securing Chiara's pack to the back of her saddle. Then silently patted her leg in farewell. Zae and Toric had already started riding. She gave Jeter a small kick, and he eagerly picked up a trot.

Chiara's home was on the opposite side of town from the bridge. Still, it would be a short ride to join the caravan. Farebrook was small. It had only one street that led from one end of town to the town green.

Trade caravans used the open area almost every month during the summer. While the caravans were in town, banners would decorate the keep that overlooked the green. Market days were a chance for everyone in town to bring out food or crafts that they had made. Villagers who knew how to play music would perform through the day. At night, people would dress in their best clothes and dance for hours.

Jeter snorted angrily and Chiara's happy memories were

forgotten. They had reached the school house. Her thoughts turned to the wyvern attack the day before. Jeter snorted again and tossed his dark mane at the smell of the wyverns. "Easy boy, there aren't any left for you to fight."

Smoke billowed up from the bonfire and darkened the sky. As they got closer, Chiara saw adults and some older children dragging wyvern carcasses to add to the fire. School had been cancelled until the bodies could be cleaned up.

Chiara glanced up to her griffin, Solandra. Seeing his large golden form flying over her made her feel safer. If it hadn't been for Cirrus and Solandra many of her friends might have died in the attack the day before. The scourge of wyverns had been bigger than any pack of wyverns anybody had ever seen. Even with their griffins' help, it had been a hard fight and many people had been injured.

"What's wrong now?" Toric asked under his breath, distracting her from her thoughts.

Chiara followed Toric's gaze. A group of ten wagons were scattered in front of the bridge. Everard, the messenger from Ash Falls, was waiting a short distance away. He was shaking his head as if puzzled by the confusion.

"I told them to line up," Toric said to no one in particular. Zae and Chiara slowed their horses as Toric urged his horse toward the center of the mess. "Graven, what's wrong? Why haven't you lined up yet?"

"No one is willing to take the lead," Graven, Toric's son, waved at the mess. The tall young man was already training to take over as the town's man-at-arms.

"The lead wagon is the most likely to be attacked," Wellend, one of the men in the group, explained. "I need my oxen to haul our harvest to market in a few weeks." Nods and mumbles of support followed the man's comment.

"I promise you, no one's going to lose their animals," Toric tried to reassure the crowd. "My son and I will ride in front. If we're attacked by wyverns we'll handle them."

"If we get ambushed by one of those… those scourges, there'll be nothing you can do," the voice of another man carried up from the center of the group.

"I made it here yesterday, all by myself," Everard pointed from the back of the crowd.

"You were on a fast horse," a wagon driver argued from another part of the crowd. "We're driving ox drawn wagons. We'll be sitting ducks."

"Toric," Chiara called in a quiet voice. The man at arms didn't hear her. "Toric," she said his name louder and cringed when everyone turned to look at her.

"What is it?" Toric turned toward her.

"The griffins will tell us if there are any wyverns around," Chiara said. Nervously licking her lips. She felt the eyes of the town's people on her. "Long before they

"Nope," Chiara grinned at the older woman. Jessilynn ran the town's only store and used to give her pieces of honey candy when she was little. The large red headed woman was known as a fair bargainer. In fact, she had donated most of the goods that the carts were hauling.

"Where are your griffins anyway?" Everard looked around.

"Up there," Chiara said, pointing at two dots circling above them.

"Blazes," Jessilynn cursed softly with a comfortable chuckle. "I get dizzy just climbing to the top of my ladder."

"Me too," Chiara laughed along with the older woman. Secretly though, she couldn't wait to try to fly with Solandra.

CHAPTER 2

Chiara shifted her seat, trying to ease her saddle sores. She glanced over at Zae who didn't look like he was feeling much better. She heard a chuckle from behind her. When she looked back she saw Jessilynn covering her smile.

"I'm sorry."

"I bet we look pretty funny," Chiara laughed.

"I've never ridden this far in my whole life," Zae moaned.

"We should be to Ash Falls

before night fall at this pace."

Chiara's vision blurred. In her mind she saw a group of eight wyverns. *Where?* The image drew farther away until she could see the line of wagons in the distance.

"Did you see that too?" Chiara asked Zae when the image faded.

"Yeah," Zae agreed. "I'll go tell Toric."

"What is it?" Jessilynn asked, her red braid whipped around as she looked at the nearby trees nervously.

"There's some wyverns up ahead," Chiara told her with a reassuring smile.

"How many?"

"Only eight," Chiara said not thinking.

"Eight!" Jessilynn gasped. Fear made her pull her oxen to a stop.

"Hey!" an angry yell came from the next wagon in line, and then the next as each one was forced to suddenly stop.

"It's alright," Chiara said trying to reassure her. "They're a long ways off. Zae and I will take care of them long before you see them."

"All by yourselves?" Everard asked doubtfully. He pushed his hat back to scratch at his balding head.

"Sure," Chiara nodded.

"Not this time," Toric said, interrupting them. Zae and Graven were behind him. "We're coming with you. There's enough of them that I'd feel better if we were there to help."

"Okay," Chiara said with a glance at Zae. He shrugged and

rolled his eyes like he'd already argued about it. They'd often hunted bigger groups of wyverns by themselves over the summer.

"Jessilynn," Toric said, turning to the woman. "Keep the wagons moving at an easy pace. If anything goes wrong we'll send someone back to warn you."

"Alright," Jessilynn hesitated, then used a long stick to tap the oxen's rumps to get them moving.

"Let's go, you three," Toric instructed the teenagers and kicked his horse into a canter.

Chiara took one last look at the wagons as they sped out of sight. Then she shifted her concentration to the image Solandra was showing her. The wyverns had moved closer to the road. This time Chiara studied the area around the creatures. It would be better if they took the wyverns by surprise. She spotted a large clump of trees that could work.

"Hold up," Zae yelled to Toric.

The man-at-arms heard him and pulled his horse to a walk. "Where are they?" He looked around like he expected the wyverns to come out of the grass under them.

"Over that way," Zae said pointing off to their left.

"Are you planning on using that clump of trees?" Chiara asked.

"Yeah," Zae agreed.

"What are you two talking about?" Toric asked, frustrated. "Which clump of trees?"

"We'll show you," Chiara assured him.

"But we should to tie the horses up here," Zae said. "So they don't give us away."

CHAPTER 3

Chiara drew her bowstring back to her ear and aimed at the wyvern furthest on the right. The green-scaled creature was hunched over their kill. It used the claws on its wings to hold the deer while it pulled off a chunk of meat. The thing was small, only about as tall as a sheep. It was probably a juvenile, but it was still deadly. Most of the other wyverns in the pack were at least a foot taller.

Toric and Graven were taking

aim at the ones they had picked. Since Zae wasn't any good at archery, he was waiting nearby. Their griffins were ready, flying high overhead.

"When I say," Toric whispered, and then waited a few seconds. "Now!"

Chiara let go of her bowstring and watched as the arrow sped towards its target. She caught her breath when she thought the wyvern was about to move. It held still just long enough for the arrow to hit the center of the creature's scaly chest. A shriek made Chiara glance over. Graven had hit his target, but Toric's wyvern had been lucky enough to move. His arrow only pierced its wing. The creature's cry alerted the pack and they were soon spotted.

Zae had been waiting for his turn. He stepped forward and stood between Chiara and the pack that was charging towards them. Toric followed his example and stood with his sword at the ready. Meanwhile his son, Graven, nocked another arrow.

Solandra and Cirrus screamed overhead. Chiara looked up to see the two large griffins diving with their wings folded. They were falling so fast she was worried they'd crash. At the last moment, they opened their wings and pulled out of their dive. Each griffin grabbed a wyvern with their talons, killing them. Chiara and Graven had enough time to take one more shot before the rest of the wyverns were on them. She saw Toric slash at a wyvern on her right. His blade easily took the thing's head off.

A cry brought Chiara's attention back to Zae who had a wyvern pinned to the ground with the point of his bill hook. With his polearm stuck in the ground, Zae was vulnerable to the wyvern flapping toward him. Chiara took aim and sent an arrow into the wyvern's neck.

"One left," Chiara told the others. Solandra dove for the last wyvern. The griffin had his talons stretched out ready to slash. Just as he was about to hit the wyvern, an arrow whooshed past Chiara's ear. "Solandra, look out!" she shouted, too late. Solandra hit the wyvern first. Then the arrow struck his feathered wing. The griffin shrieked in pain, and fell the last few feet.

"Solandra!" Chiara screamed, dashing forward to help her griffin. Toric followed her to finish off the wyvern that Solandra had been attacking.

"How is he?" Zae asked. Toric and Graven came over to help too.

"It went all the way through," Chiara said. "Why weren't you more careful, Graven?"

"I'm sorry. I didn't know Solandra was diving at it."

"It wasn't his fault," Toric defended his son. "Solandra just got in the way of his shot. It happens."

"That's never happened before when I'm shooting," Chiara told them. "Never even close."

"Never?" Toric asked surprised. "Do you tell the griffins where you're shooting?"

"I don't think so," Chiara frowned. "I've never thought about it."

"We'll figure it out later," Toric told them. "Let's take care of that wound. Chiara, hold his wing still."

Chiara did as she was told and reminded Solandra that Toric was trying to help. The first thing he did was remove the head of the arrow. The griffin screeched in pain as the shaft of the arrow slipped out of the wing.

"I think it just went through his skin." Toric gently felt along the bones in Solandra's wing. "Put some pressure on the holes and let's see if we can get it to stop bleeding." He turned to his son. "Graven, Zae, ride back to the caravan. Let them know that it's safe to keep coming. I'll wait here with Chiara so Solandra can rest."

*****

"They'll be here soon." Chiara was focused on the caravan.

Toric considered the sun. "It's close to midday. Let's start a cook fire for lunch." They were set up in the shade of a huge elm tree when the wagons pulled to a stop.

"Any trouble?" Toric asked, holding onto his son's horse as he dismounted.

"Nope," Graven told him, shaking his head. "Didn't see hide nor scale of a wyvern."

"I told you so," Chiara said coming up to them. "Cirrus said there weren't any wyverns around."

"He might not see any," Toric pointed out. "But remember there's a scourge somewhere nearby. A pack of wyverns that big just couldn't have vanished."

"Hey, how's Solandra doing?" Zae asked.

"Better," Chiara said.

"I'm really sorry," Graven apologized again.

"I know," Chiara told him. "It wasn't your fault."

"I've been talking with Chiara while you were gone," Toric explained. "I think the griffins see what she's aiming at and avoid her arrows."

"That would make sense," Zae agreed. "I was thinking about it too. I've never had a near miss when I'm swinging my bill hook either."

"Good to know," Toric nodded. "The question is, can the griffins see what we're aiming at?"

"I don't know," Chiara shrugged one shoulder.

"We'll have to try it later," Toric told them. "But we need to keep going if we're to make it to Ash Falls tonight. Do you think Solandra can fly?"

"He wants to," Chiara told him.

"Go ahead and let him," Toric said. "But if his wing hurts, tell him to land."

CHAPTER 4

"Wow," Chiara gasped. The sun was just setting as they crested the last hill. It had been an uneventful afternoon, and they'd made good time. Ahead of them was the waterfall that gave Ash Falls its name. Toric chuckled quietly next to her. She ignored him and continued to gaze at the view.

The town lay nestled at the base of a plateau. Along the ridge, Chiara could just see the edges of the ash forest. A large stream flowed over the edge of the cliff and crashed onto huge boulders at the bottom. The torrent slowed a little ways from the cliff and became a river again.

In the light of the setting sun, Chiara studied the town in front of them. Ash Falls was bigger than Farebrook. Cottages lined two streets that intersected at the town's green.

As they got closer Chiara could see evidence of the wyvern attack. Here and there holes had been torn through the thatch roofing. A shiver went down her back when she realized they were big enough for a wyvern to get through. In other places, there were claw marks on doors or window shutters. Some of the damage was so bad the shutters weren't able to close any more.

Tall buildings surrounded the green. Most of them were two stories tall with shops on the ground floor and living areas above them. Chiara noticed one business she had never seen before. It had a sign that read, 'The Bashful Bull Inn'.

"What's an inn?" Chiara asked Toric, pointing.

"An inn is a place for travelers to spend the night," Toric answered. "Ash Falls is at the crossroads of two trade routes. Wealthy traders are willing to pay to sleep in beds after long days on the road."

"Dad," Graven called to get Toric's attention. "Someone's coming."

"That's Gervase," Toric told

his son. "Ash Fall's man-at-arms."

Chiara looked at where Graven was pointing and saw two men striding toward the caravan.

"Gervase, you look like a wyvern chewed you up and spit you out," Toric said with a grin, dismounting.

"At least they spit me out," Gervase said with a grim smile. He was walking with a limp, a bandage wrapped around his thigh. There was another blood stained bandage half covering his left eye. He shook Toric's outstretched hand. "Some weren't that lucky."

"I'm sorry," Toric clasped his hand. "We're here to help. We have food 'n medicine. Where'd you like us to put them?"

"On the town green." Gervase

turned to the man next to him. "Wilhim, get one of the members of the council to pass out the food. We don't need to unload all of it tonight, but there are families that need something to eat for dinner. Also, ask Mabel to come and get the medical supplies."

"Graven, direct the wagons to the green," Toric told his son.

"How were you able to send so much?" Gervase's eyes widened when he noticed the barrels and bins of food as the wagons passed by. "That's more supplies than we had before the attack."

"Really?" Toric asked. "Why? Did you have trouble with your crops?"

"We've had wyvern attacks all summer," Gervase said. "We'd barely produced enough to make it through the winter. Then this." His eyes narrowed. "Haven't they been attacking Farebrook?"

"No, not really," Toric said and glanced sidelong at Zae and Chiara.

"How is that possible?"

"They've been hunting the wyverns with griffins," Everard walked up to them, interrupting the conversation.

"What does he mean?"

"No reason to keep them secret," Toric said with a smile. "Kids, ask your friends to land."

"Blazes," Gervase cursed when he saw Solandra landing a few minutes later. "How did you tame it?"

"It's a long story. But these two kids," and Toric nodded toward Chiara and Zae, "and their griffins have been keeping Farebrook clear of wyverns all summer. They're also how we survived an attack by a scourge yesterday."

"Yesterday?" Gervase asked stunned. "That means that there are two giant packs of wyverns."

"There were," Toric corrected him. "We killed most of the wyverns that attacked Farebrook."

"And these griffins really helped you?" Gervase looked wide eyed at the griffin.

"I've watched them do it again today," Toric told him.

"Today?" Gervase's eyes widened in surprise. "You were attacked on your way here?"

"More like we did the attacking," Zae boasted. "Cirrus and Solandra spotted them way before they could attack the caravan."

"That's another story that will have to wait," Toric said. "Right now we need a place to rest, it's been a long day."

"You're welcome to camp here on the green," Gervase told them. "But I'm sorry, you'll have to supply your own meal."

"Cirrus has that covered," Zae told them. Gervase jumped back as Zae's griffin landed nearby, a deer clutched in his front talons.

"Good job," Toric told Cirrus. "Graven, get some men and start cooking supper."

"Yes, sir," Graven smiled.

"What about the scourge?" Zae asked. "Should we start looking for them tonight?"

"How's Solandra's wing?" Toric turned to Chiara.

Chiara was walking back from checking on her friend. "It's sore."

"Then you should let him rest for the night," Toric directed them. "You four can start hunting in the morning."

CHAPTER 5

"Can you see them?" Chiara whispered.

"Yeah," Zae nodded. "They're up behind that clump of bushes."

"Oh, okay, now I see them," Chiara spotted the wyverns. She could just hear their hissing growls as they fought over what was left of a deer. Their snarls sent shivers down her spine. "So, what's the plan?"

"I was thinking about the pack we fought this morning," Zae

began to explain.

"I don't think getting ambushed by wyverns that we knew were there, is a good strategy," Chiara joked quietly. She tucked her long blond hair back behind her ear. It was funny now, but she'd been terrified when the wyverns had jumped out of the bushes right next to Zae.

"Yeah, well," Zae said, his cheeks turning red. "I meant I was thinking about how well it worked with them coming at me when they couldn't see you."

"I guess." It had been easy to hit the wyverns as they passed in front of her. The creatures had been so focused on Zae that they hadn't even realized that she was there.

"We could plan it this time.

You stay hidden in those bushes there, I'll draw them out this way."

Zae's arm gestures helped Chiara imagine how the fight would go. She nodded when it seemed like it would work.

"When do you want to try it?" Chiara glanced at the wyverns that were still eating.

"Soon as you're ready," Zae told her.

Chiara moved behind the clump of bushes Zae had pointed to. Crouching down so she was out of sight, she nocked an arrow. She nodded at Zae. Then she waited, her bow aimed at the space in front of her where they would pass her.

"Hey, uglies," Zae stepped out of hiding, waving his arms. "Over here."

A screech answered his taunt as one of the wyverns caught sight of him. The sound made Chiara's legs weak. All of her instincts were telling her to run. She drew back on her bow, her nerves as tight as the string. She had to imagine what it looked like as more growls told her that the rest of the pack had spotted Zae.

Chiara got a whiff of what smelled like a mix of rotten meat and chicken manure. She knew they must be close. Then all of a sudden she saw them. Four of the wyverns were charging Zae on the ground. The other three had taken to the air. Chiara aimed at the lead wyvern running toward Zae.

The bow string made a soft twang as she released it. Her first arrow sped toward the target. It hit with a wet sucking sound and dug deep into the wyvern's throat. The creature crumpled to the ground.

The three remaining wyverns didn't even pause as they leaped over its body. Now she could hear their claws scraping on the rocks as they ran. They were so focused on Zae they hadn't realized that they were under attack.

Chiara nocked another arrow and dropped the second wyvern. They were closing in on Zae. She reached for another arrow even before the second one had fallen. She knew that Zae was counting on her. If she didn't take out enough of them he would be overwhelmed. Zae was risking his life to give Chiara her best chance at killing the wyverns. Watching her last arrow fly through the air in a wide arc, she saw their griffins swooping down on their targets. The arrow imbedded itself into the wyvern. Its hissing shriek of pain was joined by the griffin's battle screams. She could tell through her link with Solandra that the griffins had their targets. At the same moment Zae was able to stab the last wyvern with his bill hook. He pinned it to the ground where it hissed and thrashed one last time.

"That worked great," Chiara exclaimed. Her relief that the fight was over almost made her giddy. Zae was pulling his bill hook out of the wyvern. "Did you see my shots?"

"Yeah, they were great," Zae said with a frown.

"What's wrong?" Chiara asked. "Your plan worked."

"Yeah, but you did all the work," Zae pointed out, looking around at the six other wyverns.

"But you were the one in danger," Chiara pointed out.

"I'm hungry," Zae said, changing the subject. "Let's head back to town for lunch and see how everyone else is doing."

CHAPTER 6

Zae and Chiara trudged through Ash Falls. They had sent their griffins off to rest and find food for themselves. The two friends planned to do the same.

"Well…?" Toric asked when he spotted Zae and Chiara. "Any sign of the scourge?"

"We've found so many packs," Zae said tiredly, groaning as he sat down. "We haven't killed this many wyverns since the beginning of the summer."

"No, we haven't found the scourge yet," Chiara answered Toric's question through a mouthful of food.

"Where could they be hiding?" Toric asked no one in particular.

Zae and Chiara had joined Toric and Graven in Gervase's house. The man-at-arm's home looked like an armory. Swords of all sizes hung on the wall, and a bow hung above the fire place.

Chiara took another bite of the cheese sandwich that Toric had given her. She washed it down with a gulp of cool water. They'd be out hiking the hills around Ash Falls again as soon as they had eaten.

"It's not like wyverns to hide," Gervase said, shaking his head.

"Then why can't we find

them?" Graven asked.

"Could they have gone somewhere else?" Chiara asked.

"Wyverns are territorial." Toric shook his head. "They don't go very far from their hunting grounds."

"I'm going to take some men and search some caves nearby." Gervase told them.

"Good idea," Toric said. "Where do you want Graven and me to go?"

"Why don't you follow the river," Gervase suggested. "About a mile downstream it cuts through a steep gorge. Maybe they're under the trees down there."

"What do you want us to do?" Zae asked.

"Keep doing what you're doing," Toric told him. "Let your

friends lead you to any wyverns they can find."

"That's good," Gervase nodded agreement. "But remember, if your griffins spot the scourge, stay away from it. There are too many for just you kids to take on."

*****

Chiara sighed, sinking onto a large rock along the river. She'd picked a spot along the river facing the town's green. She pulled off her boots and rubbed her aching feet. Easing her feet in to the cold water, she gasped. It was nearly sunset and they'd been hiking all day. Solandra was stretched out on the river's edge exhausted.

"They're still making supper,"

Zae flopped down next to her and handed her an apple.

"Thanks, I'm starving."

The two friends sat in silence for a while eating and watched the activity in town. A lot had been done while they'd been gone. From where she sat, Chiara could see the lighter color of the new thatch patching the roofs. She could hear the rasping sound of planers, and the pounding of hammers. Everyone she could see was busy making new doors and shutters. There was so much noise and activity she dreaded getting any closer. That's why she had picked this spot.

Nearby giggling distracted Chiara from her study of the town. Glancing over her shoulder she spotted a group of young kids coming down the road carrying empty baskets. As she watched, the boy snatched a basket from one of the little girls. He held it too high for her to reach. Chiara was about to get up to help the girl when the second girl started tickling the boy. He laughed so hard he fell to the ground.

"You can't catch me." The littlest girl grabbed her basket and dashed toward the bridge. As the girl ran past them, Solandra raised his head to see what was going on. The little girl shrieked and fell backwards. She scrambled toward the other kids on her hands and knees.

"Don't be scared," Chiara called. "He won't hurt you."

"You're the ones who tamed the griffins." The boy helped the little girl to her feet.

"I'm Zae and this is Chiara. The griffin that startled you is Solandra."

"What're your names?" Chiara asked.

"My name's Warin, and these are my little sisters Rose," he pointed to the girl who had been startled. "And Cecily."

"He's so big," Rose peered shyly from behind her brother.

"Would you like to pet him?" Chiara asked. She had already asked Solandra to stay lying down. She was worried that if he stood up the kids would be too scared.

"Can I?" Rose asked, looking up at her brother for permission.

"I guess so," Warin said. He walked forward with Rose. Cecily followed close behind them.

Chiara stood next to Solandra, stroking his feathered head to show the kids that it was safe. The youngsters took positions along the griffin's body and tentatively began petting him. Seeing them right next to Solandra made Chiara realize how big her griffin really was. Comparing his body to them she realized that he was about the size of a horse.

"Where are you three headed?" Zae asked, still soaking his feet in the river.

"Our mom sent us to get flour from the mill." Cecily pointed at the building across the river.

"We should get going," Warin reminded his younger sisters.

"Aww," the two girls whined.

"Mom will have our hides if we're not back with the flour

soon," Warin pointed out.

"I'm sure we'll see you again," Chiara told them.

"Can I pet the other one tomorrow?" The littlest one, Rose, clutched her hands in excitement.

"Sure you can," Zae told her. "Cirrus loves to be petted."

With that, the two little girls ran to catch up to their brother. Chiara smiled at their antics. It was good to see them playing even though the wyverns could still attack.

CHAPTER 7

"Are you two loaded up?" Toric asked them, coming up to where they were waiting with their horses.

"We're ready," Zae reported.

"And the Griffins are already scouting ahead," Chiara added.

"Remind them not to go too far," Toric told her. "The caves in that mountain are the most likely place for the scourge to be hiding. I don't want them facing them alone."

"Do you really think this is it?" Zae asked as Chiara warned their griffins.

"It's the only place left that is close enough and big enough," Toric lifted one shoulder in a lopsided shrug. "But who knows. These scourges are doing things we've never seen before."

"Mount up!" Gervase hollered across the town green, interrupting their conversation.

Chiara thought about where they were headed. Gervase had told them about the mountain the night before. It had enough caves for a scourge to call home. The only reason they hadn't searched it before now was because it was so far away.

The only way the hunting party could get to the caves and back before nightfall was to go by horseback. Chiara held her breath as she mounted Jeter, expecting her saddle sores to hurt. She settled onto the saddle gingerly. She sighed in relief when there was almost no pain. Giving Jeter a small kick, Chiara joined the rest of the hunting party as they headed west out of town.

Chiara realized how nervous she was when she caught herself fingering her bow for the fifth time. This was the first time she had ever had this much time to think before a fight. She made herself study the countryside around them to take her mind off of where they were going.

The path they followed wound through fields of tall grass. Dots of yellow marked late blooming flowers that covered the rolling hills. The tranquil scenery soon set her at ease and she relaxed despite her worries about the coming fight.

"That's it," Gervase told them pointing to a distant peak. "It's not far now."

The ash trees that gave Ash Falls its name slowly gave way to pine as the hunting party approached the mountain. Two hours later, Gervase called a halt at the base of the mountain. Now Chiara could see some of the caves. There wasn't any sign of wyverns.

"Alright, listen up," Gervase shouted over the murmur of conversations. "You all know your group leaders. Toric, I want you to follow the mountain around to the south. My group is going up and around the face of the mountain. The griffins haven't spotted any wyverns. That doesn't mean they aren't hiding in the caves, so stay alert."

With that, the groups split up. There was some shuffling as the riders of the hunting party reorganized into their assigned groups. But Zae and Chiara were already next to Toric. Chiara fiddled with her bow, her nerves on edge again now that they were there. Luckily it didn't take long.

The sun was nearly overhead as their group turned south. Even though it was almost winter, the sun beat down on them. Sweat trickled down Chiara's back as she wiped perspiration from her forehead.

Squinting up at the side of the mountain, Chiara searched for any sign of the scourge. It wasn't like wyverns were tidy eaters. If the creatures were there they should be able to see some remains of their meals.

Toric led them around the base of the mountain. Their path wound through open meadows and clumps of pines. Sometimes the branches of the pine trees were so low to the ground that they couldn't see more than a few feet as their horses pushed through them.

Several times Chiara thought her heart would pound out of her chest when they stumbled into different animals. They startled a few deer in one clearing. Then they flushed a group of turkeys in another. The birds squawked their objection as they erupted into the air. But that was all they found.

It was midafternoon by the time they got back to where the hunting group had split up. They didn't have to wait long before a tumble of gravel announced the arrival of Gervase's group. Chiara was hot, tired and hungry. She wasn't paying attention to what the Men-at-Arms were talking about as they waited.

An image of a girl riding a horse intruded on Chiara's day dream of a cool bath. She tried to make sense of what she was seeing. Her stomach knotted when she recognized the rider.

Where is she? In answer, the view of the girl drew back until she could see their hunting group.

"Toric!" Chiara called to get his attention.

"What is it?"

"It's Cecily, she's riding towards us," Chiara told him. "Fast."

"How far away is she?"

"Maybe an hour if her horse can keep up the pace," Chiara judged.

"Let's ride to meet her," Gervase suggested, his face grim.

That's when Chiara realized that they'd left the town unprotected. Her heart sank as images of the holes clawed in the roofs and doors flashed through her mind.

Gervase led them back toward Ash Falls. This time they pushed their horses as fast as they could. If a scourge was attacking the town, it would take too long to get there. Not giving up, she spurred Jeter to go a little faster.

Chiara used her link with Solandra to watch their progress. It seemed to take forever until the little girl finally came into view. She checked the angle of the sun and was relieved that it hadn't moved much. Gervase and Toric were the first to reach the girl as she reigned her tired horse to a stop.

"What's happened?" Gervase asked. "Is the town under attack?"

"No," Cecily shook her head, but her wide eyes still shown with fear. "My brother and sister are missing."

"What do you mean, missing?" Gervase asked.

"My sister and I took our family's sheep out to graze this

morning." Cecily began her tale. "When we were bringing them back in, we noticed that one of the pregnant ewes was missing. I told Rose that we should get help, but the ewe was her pet and she ran off looking for it. When I got home, Mom told me to find you. Then Warin ran into the woods to look for her."

Toric considered the sun. "It'll be nearly dark by the time we get back to Ash Falls."

"I know." Gervas looked at the ground and rubbed the back of his neck. He looked up at Toric with a frown. "If they aren't back by then we'll have to wait until morning to look for them."

"But that'll be too late," Cecily protested nearly in tears.

"Wait," Zae interrupted. "I have

an idea."

"What is it?" Toric asked.

"We can ride ahead on our griffins." Chiara said.

Zae nodded. "They're the best way to look for the kids anyway."

"That's impossible." Gervase dismissed their idea with a wave of his hand.

Chiara looked at Toric. He was scratching his beard but he hadn't said no, yet.

"We'll hold onto a rope around their necks." Chiara explained.

"They're as big as horses now," Zae pointed out.

"Will your griffins let you ride them?" Gervase asked doubtfully. "It takes time to break horses to ride."

"They're already landing," Chiara pointed to where their

friends were back-winging to slow their decent. "They agreed to let us ride them months ago. We've just been waiting until they were old enough."

"Graven, hand me your rope," Toric said as he dismounted from his horse. "Let's see if we can do better than just a rope around their necks to keep you kids on."

CHAPTER 8

It only took a few minutes for the three of them to come up with an idea that would work. The next problem was getting the griffins to stand still while they fitted them with their riding harnesses.

"Get your beak out of there," Chiara scolded Solandra for a second time. "Why don't you watch what they're doing to Cirrus? It's the same thing we're doing to you. That way you can see without getting your big feathered head in our way." With the griffins finally holding still, they could finish getting the harnesses on. Chiara and Zae mounted onto their backs. Then they tied themselves to the harness.

"I don't like sending you kids by yourself," Toric said looking up at them in concern. "I promised your parents I'd make sure you were safe."

"We'll be fine," Zae reassured his mentor.

"We'll find the kids and get them back to town," Chiara agreed. "We'll be back in time for dinner."

"Alright, take care of each other." Toric instructed them.

"Good luck," Graven added. Then he and his father stepped

back to give the griffins room to take off.

Chiara wouldn't admit it, but she was excited. She was worried about Warin and Rose too, but this was her chance to fly with Solandra. She'd been waiting for this moment for almost a year.

I'm ready, let's go, she told her friend in her mind.

Chiara felt Solandra's muscles bunch underneath her as he got ready to take off. She grabbed the harness and held her breath as he spread his wings. When Solandra leapt off the ground it felt like a hand was pulling her backward. His wings scooped the air to push them higher.

"Woo-hoo!" Zae cheered from her right.

Chiara glanced over to at him.

He was gripping the straps of the harness as tightly as she was, but his face was lit up with excitement. It was then that Chiara realized that she was laughing. She was smiling so wide her face was starting to hurt.

Each beat of the griffins' wings took them higher and higher into the sky. Chiara looked down and was surprised to see that the hunting party had shrunk to the size of ants below her. She had only ever seen the world like this through Solandra's eyes. Now she was able to see it for herself and it was better than she had dreamed.

Chiara was having so much fun that she forgot about where they were going. Then Solandra sent her a mental image. He had spotted the kids. Looking down

Chiara realized that they had already passed over Ash Falls. They were close to the waterfall that cascaded down the cliffs. She could just barely spot the two kids at the base of the cliff.

"They're in trouble," Zae yelled over the noise of the wind.

Chiara looked where he was pointing, but couldn't see what was wrong. Solandra let her see through his eyes and everything was suddenly much closer. She could easily spot the pack of wyverns surrounding the kids. Warin was keeping them at bay with the end of his bow.

Three, Chiara counted, spotting a fourth one impaled by an arrow a short ways away. He wouldn't be able to hold them off much longer.

Chiara spotted Rose hiding behind her brother. The little girl's arms were wrapped around a new born lamb. Its mother was nervous but refused to leave her baby's side.

An image of Solandra flashed through Chiara's thoughts. It gave her just enough time to grab onto the harness. The two griffins folded their wings and dove. Soon they were silently speeding toward the ground. The air whipped past Chiara, threatening to push her from Solandra's back. She clung to the harness with all of her strength. Tears streamed from her eyes, but she didn't shut them. Instead she watched, through squinted eyes, as the griffins attacked.

They seemed to be in an

uncontrolled fall. Chiara thought they were about to die, splattered on the ground like rotten apples. Before they hit, Solandra and Cirrus opened their wings. Their fall slowed so suddenly that Chiara's face smacked into Solandra's feathered shoulders. Her nose hit hard enough to make her see stars.

The griffins had back winged just in time to use their weight and momentum to crush the wyverns beneath their talons. Cirrus had managed to get two wyverns, one in each clawed foot. Solandra pecked at the one he had killed as if hoping it was still alive.

"I think it's dead," Chiara told her friend. A moment later Solandra gave up with a bored sigh.

A loud bleat of protest drew Chiara's attention back to the kids. Warin stood, mouth slightly agape, staring at the two griffins. Rose's grasp on the lamb was slipping. Her face was split with the widest grin, her eyes wide in surprise. The lamb was struggling to get down to follow his mom who had fled to the edge of the clearing. The ewe's fear finally winning over her maternal instincts.

"Hang on to that lamb." Chiara scrambled to untie the ropes holding her onto Solandra. "He's the only thing keeping his mom this close to the griffins."

Rose wrapped her arms around the lamb again. She blushed slightly at almost letting it go.

"I thought we were going to

die," Warin said to no one in particular. He shook his head as if he was trying to wake up.

"You're safe now," Zae jumped down from Cirrus' back. He scowled at the younger boy. "But next time you might not be that lucky."

Chiara shook her head at Zae. "There'll be time for lectures later." She watched the griffins leap into the air. She couldn't wait to try that again. With a sigh she turned to help the kids. "Let's get you back to your folks."

CHAPTER 9

The sun was dipping behind the trees that surrounded Ash Falls as Chiara and Zae led the youngsters into town. Several families had gathered in the town green. One woman spotted them and rushed to her kids.

"Warin, Rose," The woman cried scooping the kids into her arms. "Thank heavens you're alright." The lamb protested as it got squeezed between them. "What were you thinking?"

"I'm sorry, Mom," Rose's voice wavered. "But Snowball is one of our last ewes, I had to save her and her baby."

"We can replace the sheep," Rose's mother told her sternly. "I can't replace you or your brother."

"Isn't the hunting party back yet?" Chiara asked. A small crowd had gathered while Rose and her mother had been talking.

"No," an older man told her. "You're the first ones we've seen."

A griffin scream interrupted his answer. Everyone looked up at the large creatures flying overhead. They were challenging something in the sunset. At first Chiara couldn't see anything. Then she squinted and saw a dark mass blocking the glow of the setting sun.

What is it? Chiara asked Solandra. Suddenly the dark mass zoomed into focus and she gasped. "There're so many."

"That's more than was in the one that attacked Farebrook," Zae agreed.

"What're we going to do?" Chiara asked, looking around at the town's elders and children. Anyone able to fight wyvern's had gone with the hunters this morning.

"I'll be the bait," Zae told her, coming to a decision. His hand trembled as he brushed his hair back out of his eyes. "Just like we did the other day."

"But we can't do it alone," Chiara said. Then her glance landed on Warin. She remembered the wyvern he had killed defending his sister. "You're going to need more arrows.

"He'll be killed," Warin's mother clutched her son closer.

"Trust us," Zae told her. "He'll be hidden inside a house. Is there anyone else who can use a bow?"

Almost all of the town elders agreed to help, along with all of the older children. Zae had them take their places inside the houses that lined the road. He'd told them to stay hidden until the scourge was in the town.

"Are you going to be alright?" Chiara stood next to Zae in the town center.

"I'll be fine." Zae hefted his bill hook. "You should get into hiding."

Chiara left him to take her

position inside the town's grain mill. It was the closest place she take cover and still be near Zae. The mill's narrow windows made perfect archery slits.

Warin was waiting for her next to a large pile of arrows. Chiara was impressed he had gathered so many. It had only been a few minutes since they had spotted the wyverns.

"You ready?" Chiara looked at the younger boy. He nodded with his eyes wide in fear. "They'll be here soon."

Almost as if her words were a signal, a wyvern screech split the air. Nocking arrows, the two took aim through the narrow windows facing the street. There were too many wyverns to count. So many that she almost couldn't see the cottages on the other side of the road. Their plan was working. The wyverns were being drawn down the street, toward the center of town. Arrows flew from every window along the street. There were so many wyverns that the archers couldn't help but hit one of the creatures in the cross fire.

Chiara waited until the leading wyverns were directly in front of the mill house. Aiming carefully, Chiara released the bow string. Her first arrow hit the wyvern, and it fell limply to the ground. Grabbing another arrow, she took aim again. Each one of her shots needed to kill a wyvern.

Pausing as she nocked another arrow, Chiara glanced toward Zae. The leading edge of wyverns were just landing on the town green.

Zae stood with his pole arm extended in front of him. He would swing at anything that came close enough. Five wyverns paced just out of his reach, waiting for an opening to attack.

Silently, the griffins fell onto the wyverns surrounding Zae. They snatched the wyverns up in their claws, and let their momentum carry them into the sky again. Only two wyverns were left in front of Zae and he used the distraction. He quickly swung his bill hook and sliced the head off of one. Then with a quick jab, he pinned the last wyvern to the ground, killing it.

But now the scourge of wyverns knew that the griffins were there. Many of them split off from their attack on the town to pursue their natural enemies. Adult griffins could defeat several wyverns but there were just too many for her friends to handle.

The only way Chiara could help was to kill as many as she could. She aimed at a wyvern that was winging up to attack Solandra. Her arrow struck the creature full in the back and it fell to the ground. Before Chiara could celebrate, two more flew up to replace it.

CHAPTER 10

Chiara reached for the last arrow, looking at the remaining wyverns. *Make this one count.*

A scream made her look at one of the houses across the road. A large wyvern was clawing at the window the hidden archers had been using. Chiara took aim at the creature and loosed the arrow. The arrow hit the wyvern and it slumped against the wall of the home.

"That's it," Chiara said. "We're

out of arrows."

The town's defenders had done an amazing job. There were dead wyverns covering the street and a ring of destruction surrounded Zae. For a moment, Chiara thought he was doing alright. He had a few cuts that she could see but was still fighting.

While she watched, Zae lunged at another wyvern but he missed. She had seen him miss targets before and he'd always been able to recover. This time the weight of his bill hook seemed to pull him off balance. He was so tired he barely managed to stay on his feet.

Cirrus dove at the wyvern that was attacking Zae and killed it before it could get to him. The griffins were keeping him safe, but Chiara could tell they were getting tired too.

"Stay here," Chiara said. "I've got to get Zae."

Warin grabbed her arm. "I can help."

Chiara glanced back at Zae. He had dropped down to one knee. If he couldn't walk he'd be too heavy for her to carry. "Okay, but if I tell you to run, you get to safety. Got it?"

"Got it." Warin followed her out the door.

Chiara stopped in the doorway of the mill. The sound of the wyvern's growls and screeches hit them as she opened the door. It was so loud that the noise seemed to push them back. Taking a deep breath Chiara grabbed Warin's hand and started running.

Thankfully the griffins had

noticed what they were doing. With piercing screams they dove at the wyverns around Chiara and Warin. The griffins continued to protect them as they scurried to Zae.

Chiara was halfway across the green when she heard it. A low roar came from behind her. The sun was just below the tree line as she glanced toward the sunset. It was the same direction as the wyverns had come from. She expected to see some other threat. Instead, she saw warriors running out of the trees.

The men and women of the hunting party had returned. Toric and Gervase led the charge. Villagers armed with swords and pole arms attacked the wyverns that had landed. Behind them, archers knelt so that they could get a better angle on the wyverns that were flying over the town's roofs.

"They're back!" Chiara turned to see if Zae had noticed the hunting party. She gasped when she saw that her friend was down on his hands and knees. Turning back to the hunters, she waved her arms to get their attention. Toric caught sight of her and yelled something to Gervase. The two men began fighting their way toward the kids.

"Take his other side," Chiara told Warin when they got to Zae. As they helped him to stand, Zae's bill hook toppled to the ground. It had been the only thing holding him up.

Suddenly an image of a wyvern diving at her head, flashed in

Chiara's mind. "Duck!" she cried.

The three of them sprawled on the ground. Chiara heard a grunt of effort and recognized the sodden thwack of a sword. A dismembered wyvern crashed to the ground beside her with a wet thud. Chiara looked up to see Toric standing over her. Gervase was standing guard on the other side of Zae's unconscious form.

"What are you waiting for, an invitation?" Gervase asked with a wicked grin.

"You kids get back inside," Toric told them. "We'll cover you."

Without a second thought, Chiara and Warin half carried, half dragged Zae back to the mill. The sounds of wyvern growls and screeches followed them as they ran. Occasionally the sounds cut off suddenly as one of the Man-at-Arms killed a creature.

*****

It seemed to Chiara that the wyvern attack was over quickly once the town's hunting party appeared. She'd just finished caring for Zae when Toric came striding through the mill door.

"How's he doing?" The Man-at-Arms knelt down next to her.

"He's got a few cuts." Chiara wiped her brow with her shirt sleeve. "Nothing that won't heal."

"I'm mostly just exhausted." Zae tried to prop himself up onto his elbow but quickly gave up. "Never had to fight so long before."

"Is it safe?" Warin asked. "I need to find my mom. She's probably worried."

"The town's clear." Toric nodded once. "I told her that you were all right, but I'm sure she'd like to see for herself."

"How's the town doing?" Chiara asked as Warin hurried out.

Toric sighed. "There's a little more damage to the houses. But it looks like most of them were so interested in getting to Zae they didn't waste time trying to get into the homes."

"Our plan worked better than we thought it would," Zae grinned smugly.

"You're lucky it did," Toric growled. "If either of you'd been hurt, I'd never forgive myself."

CHAPTER 11

Chiara woke from the pain of her shoulder digging into the hard wood floor. It took her a moment to remember why they weren't in their tent on the town's green. The town might not have been damaged very much, but their wagons and tents had been shredded by the wyverns. So the people from Farebrook had spent the night in the inn.

Snoring from the darkness

around her told her that others were still asleep. In the early morning gloom Chiara could just see that Zae's bed roll was empty. She quietly pulled on her shoes and sneaked out of the room.

The bright morning sun seemed out of place with the grisly scene that met her as she stepped outside. The people of Ash Falls were throwing the dead wyverns onto fires that had been lit along the road. The smoke smelled horrible, but it was the quickest way to get rid of the bodies. Turning away, Chiara tried to spot Zae or Toric. She found them on the town green talking to Gervase and the Ash Falls town council.

"We'll be able to finish repairing the town ourselves," Chiara heard one of the elders say as she walked up to the group.

"Are you as stiff as I am?" Zae whispered to Chiara when he saw her.

"Just through my shoulders. You?"

"My whole body aches," Zae groaned.

"I hate leaving you with this mess," Toric said.

"You and your town have more than helped us," Gervase told him, his voice low. "If you hadn't been here when that scourge hit yesterday, we would have been wiped out."

"Do you think another one will come?" an older woman asked the two Men-at-arms.

"We don't know." Gervase shook his head.

"But we've come up with a few ideas that'll help protect our towns this winter," Toric told them. "They shouldn't be too hard to build."

"Gervase!" a young man called running up to the group. "You have to come see this!"

"What is it lad?" Gervase put a steadying hand on the boy's shoulder as he panted for breath.

"We don't know." The young man told them between breaths. "You'll have to see it yourself."

"Show us," a council member instructed him.

The whole group followed the young man back the way he had come. On the far side of town, a clump of villagers was milling around. They were gesturing toward a dead wyvern that was being guarded by an older man. It looked like the horrible creature had been dragged a short way before being dropped.

"Father," The young man called to the man standing over the creature. "I brought Gervase like you told me."

"Wilhim, what's the problem?" Gervase asked as the villagers moved aside to let the town council get closer.

"My son noticed something different about this one." Wilhim bent over and he lifted the wyvern's wing. "We thought you should see it."

The wyvern at Wilhim's feet was larger than most Chiara had seen, but not unusually big. Then her gaze fell on the creature's shoulder. Three stripes of paint, red, green and yellow, were clearly visible.

"What do you think it means?" Warin's mother asked from the crowd that was gathering.

"I'm not sure," Gervase scratched his chin, deep in thought.

"It's a big one," Toric pointed out. "It could have been the leader of the scourge."

Gervase nodded. "I've heard of armies that were so large the commanders had to name the different regiments just to keep them straight."

"When I was a child there was a fairy tale of a stone that could control wyverns." The elder clutched her shawl tighter and looked toward the forest fearfully. "You don't think someone has made an army of wyverns do you?"

"We don't know that," Gervase softened his voice reassuringly. "But I think we should report this to King Trillion. He'll know what it means."

"Good idea," Toric agreed. "I'll send word if we think of any other ways to improve our town's defensives."

"Same here," Gervase assured his friend. "Ash Falls owes you and your town a great debt."

"Glad we could help, old friend," Toric clasped arms with his old friend in farewell. Then led Chiara and Zae back toward the Farebrook wagon train.

"Do you think there could be an army of wyverns?" Behind them Chiara could hear the Ash

Falls' town council calling for Everard to get ready to ride. They were sending him to the capital city, Maralon, and King Trillion.

"I hope not," Toric said, putting his arms around the two friends. "But I feel better knowing that you and your griffins can help. Now let's get going. I'm looking forward to sleeping in my own bed tonight."

"Hey you two," Jessilynn called from the seat of her wagon. "Need a ride?"

"I'm okay," Chiara told her. "I'll ride Jeter."

"Zae, you should ride with Jessilynn." Toric held up his hand to interrupt Zae's objection. "You need to rest."

"Come on," Jessilynn urged Zae. "There's no shame in resting after what you did yesterday."

*****

Chiara patted her horse's neck. Most of the horses and oxen from Farebrook were unhurt. They had broken out of their corral and fled to safety. But her old war horse had stood and fought. Toric had spotted Jeter during the battle. The two had fought the wyverns side by side. He had told Chiara that Jeter had battled as well as any young war horse. Together they had survived the wyvern attack with only a few scrapes.

"Hurry up," Toric bellowed to be heard over the noise of the caravan loading up. "We've got a long ride ahead of us."

Chiara finished tying her

bedroll to her saddle and mounted. She rode to catch up to Jessilynn's wagon. The store keeper had taken the lead position again.

Jessilyn motioned for Chiara to be quiet as she pulled Jeter to a walk next to the wagon. The woman nodded back over her shoulder. Chiara glanced into the bed of the wagon and smiled. Zae was asleep on a pile of empty canvas sacks. He had been trying to hide it but the wyvern attack must have taken a lot out of him.

The ride home was peaceful. Solandra and Cirrus couldn't find any wyverns. The slow sway of Jeter's walk and the warm sun on her back were so relaxing. Chiara soon found herself dosing off in the saddle.

Toric rode up next to Chiara,

startling her awake. He spotted Zae sleeping and chuckled then glanced knowingly at her. "How are you holding up?"

"My arms and shoulders are sore."

"I bet."

"Guess I need to practice more." Chiara grinned wryly.

"We all do," Toric agreed.

The wagon caravan was just reaching the top of a hill. With a jolt of surprise Chiara realized she recognized the place. Sure enough, Chiara saw the bridge that marked the edge of town as they rounded the next bend in the road. But something had changed. A large barn was being built. Chiara recognized her neighbors as they called to each other, announcing the caravan's return.

"What's going on?"

"Grimald wanted your griffins close to town," Toric reminded her. He laughed when Chiara's jaw dropped in shock.

"Zae! Zae, wake up!"

"What?" Zae asked, startled into sitting bolt upright. He moaned in pain when his muscles objected.

"Look," Chiara commanded, pointing toward the barn. Zae followed Chiara's outstretched arm. His eyes widened in surprise.

"It's not in the center of town like I had asked," Toric admitted. "But there's is a lot more room for a griffin aerie over here."

At that moment a cheer went up as the townsfolk came out to greet the caravan. In the front of the crowd, Chiara saw her father waving at her, a huge smile lit up his face. Chiara leapt off Jeter and ran to his outstretched arms.

"Welcome home," Marsh said hugging her.

"What is it?" Zae rubbed his eyes.

"An aerie for your griffins," Toric said with a patient grin.

"And it's almost ready," Grimald smiled. He'd been the most supportive member of the town council.

"Just in time too." Esmerelda pulled her shawl up onto her shoulders. As the only woman on the council she was like the town's grandmother. "If my bones are right, we're in for an early snow."

"You mean our griffins will have a safe place to stay this winter?" Chiara could hardly believe it.

Toric held up a hand. "But it won't be all fun and games. You and your griffins have a lot of training ahead of you. We need to make sure we're ready just in case there is an army of wyverns out there."

ABOUT THE AUTHOR

Janet spent many years as a teacher and center director for children with special needs. Recently she has been given the opportunity to stay at home. This has allowed her to spend more time with her wonderful daughters, and it also has let her follow her passion for writing.

Made in the USA
Columbia, SC
18 March 2022

57416835R00069